Terry
Jones

The Dragon on the Roof

PENGUIN BOOKS

PENGUIN BOOKS

Published by the Penguin Group
Penguin Books Ltd, 27 Wrights Lane, London W8 5TZ, England
Penguin Books USA Inc., 375 Hudson Street, New York, New York 10014, USA
Penguin Books Australia Ltd, Ringwood, Victoria, Australia
Penguin Books Canada Ltd, 10 Alcorn Avenue, Toronto, Ontario, Canada M4V 3B2
Penguin Books (NZ) Ltd, 182–190 Wairau Road, Auckland 10, New Zealand

Penguin Books Ltd, Registered Offices: Harmondsworth, Middlesex, England

First published in *Fantastic Stories* by Pavilion Books Limited 1992
Published in Puffin Books 1994

This collection published in Penguin Books 1996
3 5 7 9 10 8 6 4 2

Set in 11.5/13.5pt Bembo Monotype
Typeset by Datix International Limited, Bungay, Suffolk
Printed in England by Clays Ltd, St Ives plc

Contents

1   The Dragon on the Roof   1

2   Mack and Mick   15

3   Tom and the Dinosaur   29

4   Nicobobinus and the Doge of Venice   44

The Dragon on the Roof

A long time ago, in a remote part of China, a dragon once flew down from the mountains and settled on the roof of the house of a rich merchant.

The merchant and his wife and family and servants were, of course, terrified out of their wits. They looked out of the windows and could see the shadows of the dragon's wings stretching out over the ground below them. And when they looked up, they could see his great yellow claws sticking into the roof above them.

'What are we going to do?' cried the merchant's wife.

'Perhaps it'll be gone in the morning,' said the merchant. 'Let's go to bed and hope.'

So they all went to bed and lay there shivering and shaking. And nobody slept a wink all night. They just lay there listening to the sound of the dragon's leathery wings beating on the walls behind their beds, and the scraping of the dragon's scaly belly on the tiles above their heads.

The next day, the dragon was still there, warming its 1

tail on the chimney-pot. And no one in the house dared to stick so much as a finger out of doors.

'We can't go on like this!' cried the merchant's wife. 'Sometimes dragons stay like that for a thousand years!'

So once again they waited until nightfall, but this time the merchant and his family and servants crept out of the house as quiet as could be. They could hear the dragon snoring away high above them, and they could feel the warm breeze of his breath blowing down their necks, as they tiptoed across the lawns. By the time they got half-way across, they were so frightened that they all suddenly started to run. They ran out of the gardens and off into the night. And they didn't stop running until they'd reached the great city, where the king of that part of China lived.

The next day, the merchant went to the King's palace. Outside the gates was a huge crowd of beggars and poor people and ragged children, and the rich merchant had to fight his way through them.

'What d'you want?' demanded the palace guard.

'I want to see the King,' exclaimed the merchant.

2   'Buzz off!' said the guard.

'I don't want charity!' replied the merchant. 'I'm a rich man!'

'Oh, then in you go!' said the guard.

So the merchant entered the palace, and found the King playing Fiddlesticks with his Lord High Chancellor in the Council Chamber. The merchant fell on his face in front of the King, and cried: 'O Great King! Favourite Of His People! Help me! The Jade Dragon has flown down from the Jade Dragon Snow Mountain, and has alighted on my roof-top, O Most Beloved Ruler Of All China!'

The King (who was, in fact, extremely unpopular) paused for a moment in his game and looked at the merchant, and said: 'I don't particularly like your hat.'

So the merchant, of course, threw his hat out of the window, and said: 'O Monarch Esteemed By All His Subjects! Loved By All The World! Please assist me and my wretched family! The Jade Dragon has flown down from the Jade Dragon Snow Mountain, and is, at this very moment, sitting on my roof-top, and refuses to go away!'

The King turned again, and glared at the merchant, and said: 'Nor do I much care for your trousers.'

So the merchant, naturally, removed his trousers and threw them out of the window.

'Nor,' said the King, 'do I really approve of anything you are wearing.'

So, of course, the merchant took off all the rest of his clothes, and stood there stark naked in front of the King, feeling very embarrassed.

'*And* throw them out of the window!' said the King.

So the merchant threw them out of the window. At which point, the King burst out into the most unpleasant laughter. 'It must be your birthday!' he cried, 'because you're wearing your birthday suit!' and he collapsed on the floor helpless with mirth. (You can see why he wasn't a very popular king.)

Finally, however, the King pulled himself together and asked: 'Well, what do you want? You can't stand around here stark naked you know!'

'Your Majesty!' cried the merchant. 'The Jade Dragon has flown down from the Jade Dragon Snow Mountain and is sitting on my roof-top!'

The King went a little green about the gills when he heard this, because nobody particularly likes having a dragon in their kingdom.

'Well, what do you expect me to do about it?' replied the King. 'Go and read it a bedtime story?'

'Oh no! Most Cherished Lord! Admired And Venerated Leader Of His People! No one would expect you to read bedtime stories to a dragon. But I was hoping you might find some way of . . . getting rid of it?'

'Is it a big dragon?' asked the King.

'It is. Very big,' replied the merchant.

'I was afraid it would be,' said the King. 'And have you tried asking it — politely — if it would mind leaving of its own accord?'

'First thing we did,' said the merchant.

'Well, in that case,' replied the King, '. . . tough luck!'

Just at that moment there was a terrible noise from outside the palace. 'Ah! It's here!' cried the King, leaping onto a chair. 'The dragon's come to get us!'

'No, no, no,' said the Lord High Chancellor. 'That is nothing to be worried about. It is merely the poor people of your kingdom groaning at your gates, because they have not enough to eat.'

'Miserable wretches!' cried the King. 'Have them all beaten and sent home.'

'Er . . . many of them have no homes to go to,' replied the Chancellor.

'Well then — obviously — just have them beaten!' 5

exclaimed the King. 'And sent somewhere else to groan.'

But just then there was an even louder roar from outside the palace gates.

'*That's* the dragon!' exclaimed the King, hiding in a cupboard.

'No,' said the Chancellor, 'that is merely the rest of your subjects demanding that you resign the crown.'

At this point, the King sat on his throne and burst into tears. 'Why does nobody like me?' he cried.

'Er . . . may I go and put some clothes on?' asked the merchant.

'Oh! Go and jump out of the window!' replied the King.

Well, the merchant was just going to jump out of the window (because, of course in those days, whenever a king told you to do something, you always did it) when the Lord High Chancellor stopped him and turned to the King and whispered: 'Your Majesty! It may be that this fellow's dragon could be just what we need!'

'Don't talk piffle,' snapped the King. '*Nobody* needs a dragon!'

'On the contrary,' replied the Chancellor, '*you* 6 need one right now. Nothing, you know, makes a king more popular with his people than getting rid of a dragon for them.'

'You're right!' exclaimed the King.

So there and then he sent for the Most Famous Dragon-Slayer In The Land, and had it announced that a terrible dragon had flown down from the Jade Dragon Snow Mountain and was threatening their kingdom.

Naturally everyone immediately forgot about being hungry or discontented. They fled from the palace gates and hid themselves away in dark corners for fear of the dragon.

Some days later, the Most Famous Dragon-Slayer In The Whole Of China arrived. The King ordered a fabulous banquet in his honour. But the Dragon-Slayer said: 'I never eat so much as a nut, nor drink so much as a thimbleful, until I have seen my dragon, and know what it is I have to do.'

So the merchant took the Dragon-Slayer to his house, and they hid in an apricot tree to observe the dragon.

'Well? What d'you think of it?' asked the merchant.

But the Dragon-Slayer said not a word.

'Big, isn't it?' said the merchant.

But the Dragon-Slayer remained silent. He just sat there in the apricot tree, watching the dragon.

'How are you going to kill it?' inquired the merchant eagerly.

But the Dragon-Slayer didn't reply. He climbed down out of the apricot tree, and returned to the palace. There he ordered a plate of eels and mint, and he drank a cup of wine.

When he had finished, the King looked at him anxiously and said: 'Well? What are you going to do?'

The Dragon-Slayer wiped his mouth and said: 'Nothing.'

'Nothing?' exclaimed the King. 'Is this dragon so big you're frightened of it?'

'I've killed bigger ones,' replied the Dragon-Slayer, rubbing his chest.

'Is it such a fierce dragon you're scared it'll finish you off?' cried the King.

'I've dispatched hundreds of fiercer ones,' yawned the Dragon-Slayer.

'Then has it hotter breath?' demanded the King. 'Or sharper claws? Or bigger jaws? Or what?'

8   But the Dragon-Slayer merely shut his eyes and

said: 'Like me, it's old and tired. It has come down from the mountains to die in the East. It's merely resting on that roof-top. It'll do no harm, and, in a week or so, it will go on its way to the place where dragons go to die.'

Then the Dragon-Slayer rolled himself up in his cloak and went to sleep by the fire.

But the King was furious.

'This is no good!' he whispered to the Lord High Chancellor. 'It's not going to make me more popular if I leave this dragon sitting on that man's roof-top. It needs to be killed!'

'I agree,' replied the Lord High Chancellor. 'There's nothing like a little dragon-slaying to get the people onto your side.'

So the King sent for the Second Most Famous Dragon-Slayer In The Whole Of China, and said: 'Listen! I want you to kill that dragon, and I won't pay you unless you do!'

So the Second Most Famous Dragon-Slayer In The Whole Of China went to the merchant's house and hid in the apricot tree to observe the dragon. Then he came back to the palace, and ordered a plate of pork and beans, drank a flask of wine, and said to 9 the King: 'It's a messy business killing dragons. The fire from their nostrils burns the countryside, and their blood poisons the land so that nothing will grow for a hundred years. And when you cut them open, the smoke from their bellies covers the sky and blots out the sun.'

But the King said: 'I want that dragon killed. Mess or no mess!'

But the Second Most Famous Dragon-Slayer In The Whole Of China replied: 'Best to leave this one alone. It's old and on its way to die in the East.'

Whereupon the King stamped his foot, and sent for the Third Most Famous Dragon-Slayer In The Whole Of China, and said: 'Kill me that dragon!'

Now the Third Most Famous Dragon-Slayer In The Whole Of China also happened to be the most cunning, and he knew just why it was the King was so keen to have the dragon killed. He also knew that if he killed the dragon, he himself would become the First Dragon-Slayer In The Whole Of China instead of only the Third. So he said to the King: 'Nothing easier, Your Majesty. I'll kill that dragon straight away.'

Well, he went to the merchant's house, climbed the apricot tree and looked down at the dragon. He could see it was an old one and weary of life, and he congratulated himself on his good luck. But he told the King to have it announced in the market square that the dragon was young and fierce and very dangerous, and that everyone should keep well out of the way until after the battle was over.

When they heard this, of course, the people were even more frightened, and they hurried back to their hiding places and shut their windows and bolted their doors.

Then the Dragon-Slayer shouted down from the apricot tree: 'Wake up, Jade Dragon! For I have come to kill you!'

The Jade Dragon opened a weary eye and said: 'Leave me alone, Dragon-Slayer. I am old and weary of life. I have come down from the Jade Dragon Snow Mountain to die in the East. Why should you kill me?'

'Enough!' cried the Dragon-Slayer. 'If you do not want me to kill you, fly away and never come back.'

The Jade Dragon opened its other weary eye and looked at the Dragon-Slayer. 'Dragon-Slayer! You know I am too weary to fly any further. I have settled 11 here to rest. I shall do no one any harm. Let me be.'

But the Dragon-Slayer didn't reply. He took his bow and he took two arrows, and he let one arrow fly, and it pierced the Jade Dragon in the right eye. The old creature roared in pain, and tried to raise itself up on its legs, but it was too old and weak, and it fell down again on top of the house, crushing one of the walls beneath its weight.

Then the Dragon-Slayer fired his second arrow, and it pierced the Jade Dragon in the left eye, and the old creature roared again and a sheet of fire shot out from its nostrils and set fire to the apricot tree.

But the Dragon-Slayer had leapt out of the tree and onto the back of the blinded beast, as it struggled to its feet, breathing flames through its nostrils and setting fire to the countryside all around.

It flapped its old, leathery wings, trying to fly away, but the Dragon-Slayer was hanging onto the spines on its back, and he drove his long sword deep into the dragon's side. And the Jade Dragon howled, and its claws ripped off the roof of the merchant's house, as it rolled over on its side and its blood gushed out onto the ground.

And everywhere the dragon's blood touched the
12 earth, the plants turned black and withered away.

Then the Dragon-Slayer took his long sword and cut open the old dragon's fiery belly, and a black cloud shot up into the sky and covered the sun.

When the people looked out of their hiding places, they thought the night had fallen, the sky was so black. All around the city they could see the countryside burning, and the air stank with the smell of the dragon's blood. But the King ordered a great banquet to be held in the palace that night, and he paid the Dragon-Slayer half the money he had in his treasury.

And when the people heard that the dragon had been killed, they cheered and clapped and praised the King because he had saved them from the dragon.

When the merchant and his wife and children returned to their house, however, they found it was just a pile of rubble, and their beautiful lawns and gardens were burnt beyond repair.

And the sun did not shine again in that land all that summer, because of the smoke from the dragon's belly. What is worse, nothing would grow in that kingdom for a hundred years, because the land had been poisoned by the dragon's blood.

★

But the odd thing is, that although the people were now poorer than they ever had been, and scarcely ever had enough to eat or saw the sun, every time the King went out they cheered him and clapped him and called him: 'King Chong The Dragon-Slayer', and he was, from that time on, the most popular ruler in the whole of China for as long as he reigned and long after.

And the Third Most Famous Dragon-Slayer In The Whole Of China became the First, and people never tired of telling and retelling the story of his fearful fight with the Jade Dragon from the Jade Dragon Snow Mountain.

What do you think of that?

Mack and Mick

ONCE upon a time there were two brothers who could never agree about anything. They argued about what to have for breakfast. They argued about what to have for lunch. They even argued about which side of the bed they should sleep on.

One day Mack said to Mick: 'I can't stand living with you another day. I'm leaving!'

'No you're not!' exclaimed Mick. 'I can't stand living with *you* another day. *I'm* the one that's leaving!'

Well, they argued and they argued and they argued about which one of them was to leave, but they just couldn't agree. So, in the end, they both left.

They marched along the road that led to the great wide world, and when they reached the crossroads, Mick turned to Mack and said: 'Goodbye, Mack. I'm taking this road that leads to the sea.'

'No you're not!' shouted Mack. 'That's my road! You'll have to take the road to the hills.'

Well, they stood there arguing for about an hour, but they couldn't agree about which road the other was taking. So in the end, they both set off along the same road. And pretty soon they came to the sea. 15

'Ah!' said Mick. 'I can't wait to put an ocean between us two.'

'Neither can I,' said Mack.

When they got to the harbour, however, they found there was only one ship due to sail.

Could they agree which of them was to take it? No, of course they couldn't.

'I was the first to say I wanted to put an ocean between us,' said Mick.

'But I was the first to say I wanted to leave!' exclaimed Mack. So they stood on the quay, and they argued and they argued and they argued – until they saw the ship weighing its anchor, and they both had to leap aboard – otherwise they'd both have missed it.

As soon as they got on board they started arguing again, and they didn't stop once.

Their crewmates quickly grew tired of them.

'Don't you two ever agree about anything?' the other sailors asked.

'No,' said Mack and Mick together. 'Never!' And they carried on arguing about which of them felt the more seasick.

Eventually the Captain could stand it no longer, 16 and he made them sleep down in the hold of the ship, away from the rest of the crew.

But, even down in the hold, the entire ship's company could still hear Mack and Mick arguing and arguing and arguing as bad as ever.

So the Captain hauled them up on deck in front of the whole crew, and said: 'We are all sick and tired of your constant bickering. It sets our teeth on edge all day, and it keeps us awake all night. So here's what I'm going to do. Either you two stop arguing, or I'm going to throw you off the ship at the next desert island we come to.'

Mack immediately turned to Mick. 'See?' he said. 'This is all your fault.'

'What are you talking about?' exclaimed Mick. 'I wouldn't be arguing if it weren't for you! It's all *your* fault.'

And they were taken down into the hold again still arguing and arguing.

Well, the ship sailed on for seven days and seven nights, until one morning the lookout shouted: 'Land ahead!'

The Captain looked through his telescope and saw a desert island on the horizon. Once again he summoned Mack and Mick up onto the deck in 17 front of the whole crew, and he said: 'I'll give you one last chance. If you can keep yourselves from arguing as long as that desert island is in sight, you can stay on board. But if you have so much as one argument, I'll throw you overboard, and you'll have to live out the rest of your lives on that island.'

Well, Mack looked at Mick, and Mick looked at Mack. Then Mack said: 'Well, Mick, if anyone starts an argument – it'll be you.'

'That's a laugh, Mack!' exclaimed Mick. 'You're much more likely to start an argument than I am!'

And with that, of course, they started arguing again, and they didn't stop until the ship reached the desert island, and the two of them were thrown overboard and they had to swim for the shore.

Mack and Mick stood on the shore of the desert island, and watched their ship disappear over the horizon.

'Well this is a pretty how's yer father!' said Mack. 'We try to get away from each other . . .'

'And we end up marooned together on a desert island,' said Mick.

'Exactly,' said Mack.

★

There wasn't much to eat on that desert island. For breakfast they managed to find two clams, so they ate one each. For lunch they managed to catch a dodo (I'm afraid it was the last one). Normally they would have argued about whether to roast or boil it, but as they didn't have any pots or pans they had no choice. They stuck it on a stick, and held it over the fire. And it tasted pretty good.

As night began to fall, they broke branches off a tree and made themselves a rough shelter by the beach. There they sat together, looking out into the night sea, hoping their ship would return to pick them up. But it didn't. And they fell asleep, trying to remember the names of the flowers that grew in their garden back home.

The next day, they searched the island and found a sparkling stream of fresh water. There they decided to build a house. Then they lit a fire at the top of the nearby hill to attract the attention of any ship that might pass by.

'We must make sure we keep it burning . . .' said Mick.

'Day and night,' said Mack.

But that night, as they sat down to a meal of fresh fish, they heard the wind begin to blow.

'Looks like there's going to be a storm,' said Mick.

'You're right,' said Mack. 'We'd better tie the roof on.'

So they tied the roof down with creepers from the forest, as the wind blew stronger and fiercer. Then the rain began to lash the island. Before long, Mick and Mack were cowering in their log house, listening to the thunder breaking over their heads, and watching bolts of lightning striking out of the sky.

Suddenly there was a terrible noise and the sound of breaking branches.

'Run!' cried Mick

'I am!' cried Mack.

And they ran as hard as they could out into the storm, just as a huge tree came crashing down on their log house, smashing it to pieces.

Still the wind blew even fiercer, and the rain lashed across their backs, and the water ran down their faces like sheets of tears.

'We must find shelter!' said Mick.

'Over there!' cried Mack. And they started

running towards a cave. They reached the cave just

as the wind began to turn into a hurricane. It blew away the remnants of their house as if it had been matchwood.

The lightning hit tree after tree, and fire swept across the island. Mack and Mick trembled, holding onto each other in the safety of the cave.

As day broke, the storm subsided, but as it did, their troubles redoubled. They awoke to a roar that made their blood run cold.

Mack and Mick both sat bolt upright, and stared in horror, for there in the mouth of the cave was a huge monster with a head as big as its own body. When it opened its jaws and roared again, both Mack and Mick thought they were going to tumble into it – its throat seemed so vast and deep.

The monster advanced into the cave, and looked from Mack to Mick and from Mick to Mack.

Mack backed away towards one side of the cave, and Mick backed towards the other, as the terrible creature took another step further into the cave. First it turned towards Mick and showed its razor-sharp teeth. Then it turned towards Mack and stretched out a razor-sharp claw.

'It can't make up its mind which of us looks tastiest!' cried Mick.

'Well let's not give it the chance to find out!' shouted Mack.

'Ready?' shouted Mick.

'Ready!' screamed Mack. And they both together sprinted for the entrance of the cave as fast as fear could take them. First the monster darted towards Mick, then it turned towards Mack, but by then Mack was out of the cave, and so was Mick!

'See you on the other side of the island!' shouted Mick.

'Right!' yelled Mack. And they both ran off in opposite directions, and the monster stood roaring in the cave mouth, hopping from one foot to the other, unable to decide whether to chase after Mick or chase after Mack.

So it was that Mack and Mick found themselves on separate sides of the island.

Mack found himself amongst quicksands and deep dark bogs that nearly sucked him down on several occasions . . . until he had the idea of tying branches to his feet so that he didn't sink in.

Mick found himself in a dark forest, infested with wild wolves. He armed himself as best he could with a stout stick and a knife, and pursued his way. But he could hear the wolves following him, and he could see their eyes glinting in the blackness of the forest.

Mick wished he had Mack with him to give him courage. And Mack wished he had Mick with him to help him every time he fell into a bog.

At length, however, they met up together on the other side of the island.

'Thank goodness!' cried Mick.

'It's good to see you!' cried Mack.

But no sooner had they hugged each other and done a little dance of joy, than an even worse calamity befell them!

They heard a terrible explosion above, and they looked up – in time to see the top blow off the volcano in the centre of the island and flames begin to shoot up into the sky. A great cloud of soot shot up into the air and covered the sun. The next minute, they saw molten rock bubbling up over the rim of the crater and down the sides of the mountain towards them.

'The sea!' cried Mack.

'Here we go again!' yelled Mick, and they both plunged into the sea, and started to swim . . . But 23 even as they hit the water, the white-hot molten lava flowed over the shore.

And they had swum no further than the shadow of the mountain at mid-morn, when the lava reached the sea. The air was filled with an ear-splitting hiss, and the island disappeared in a cloud of steam, as the water started to bubble.

'Help!' yelled Mick. 'The sea's boiling!'

'We'll be cooked – like the ogre in the next story!' cried Mack. And they both swam as hard as they could, until – as fate would have it – they reached cooler water. But the smiles on their faces quickly disappeared as they looked around them:

'Sharks!' screamed Mick.

'I don't believe it!' screamed Mack. But sure enough, they could see sharks circling all around them.

'Look out!' screamed Mack. 'Here comes one!'

'What a way to go!' yelled Mack, 'After all we've been through!'

But, just at that very moment, white-hot ash started to fall out of the sky.

'Dive!' yelled Mick. And the two brothers dived, while the hot ash fell on the sharks, and the sharks were so confused they thrashed the sea, and then turned on their tails and swam off.

Some time later, Mack and Mick found themselves clinging to a tree trunk, on which they drifted for two days and two nights. On the third day, however, the breeze blew them onto a little sandy island with two trees in the middle of it.

They lay there gasping, and wondered what else could possibly happen to them, until they both fell asleep from exhaustion, and didn't wake up until the next day.

When they opened their eyes they blinked and looked again, but – sure enough – they could see something on the horizon.

'It's a sail!' exclaimed Mick.

'We're saved!' exclaimed Mack. And the two of them jumped around the little island for joy.

But as the sail got closer, they began to realize it was a very strange sail indeed. In the first place it was big – bigger than any sail either of them had ever seen. The second strange thing about it was that it appeared to be made out of fish-skins, for one side was plain and the other was covered in silver scales. But – without a shadow of doubt – the very strangest 25 thing about the sail was the fact that there was no ship under it. It was simply a giant sail of fish-skins, flying across the water.

And when it reached the island, something even stranger happened. It blew over the heads of Mack and Mick, until it reached half-way across the little island, and there the two trees caught it in their palms – as if they'd been hands – and held it tight.

The sail of fish-skins billowed out as the wind filled it once more, and then *the strangest thing of all happened* . . . The island itself began to move . . . It started to glide across the water like a ship – blown by the wind caught in its fish-skin sail.

Mack and Mick were so surprised and so terrified all at the same time that they held onto each other tight.

Well, the wind blew the sail, and the island sped through the seas until finally they saw ahead of them the shoreline of their own country. As they approached, the wind died down, and the little island started to sink beneath the waves, so 26 Mack and Mick both had to swim for it, until they arrived back at the harbour from which they had first set out.

Mack and Mick crawled ashore, and as they did so they heard a voice. There standing on a rock, was the Captain of the ship in which they'd first sailed.

'Well?' he said. 'What happened to you?'

Mack and Mick looked at each other and said: 'We've been *bored stiff!*'

And they told the Captain their adventures.

'What!' exclaimed the Captain, when they'd finished. 'Your house was destroyed by a typhoon! You were attacked by a monster! Beset by quicksands and wild beasts! You were caught under an erupting volcano! Attacked by sharks! And brought home by a magic sail! How can you possibly call that "boring"?'

'Tell him,' said Mack.

'No, you tell him,' said Mick.

'Well,' they both said together, 'we were so hard put to it that we didn't have time for a single argument!'

'But that's marvellous!' exclaimed the Captain.

'No it isn't!' replied Mack and Mick. 'Because the one thing we learnt is that we *like* arguing!'

And with that, the two brothers took their leave of the Captain, and made their way back home.

There they continued arguing to their hearts' content.

After all, the world would be a very dull place indeed if we all agreed about absolutely everything, wouldn't it?

Tom and the Dinosaur

A small boy named Tom once noticed strange noises coming from the old woodshed that stood at the very bottom of his garden.

One noise sounded a bit like his Great Aunt Nelly breathing through a megaphone. There was also a sort of scraping, rattling noise, which sounded a bit like someone rubbing several giant tiddlywinks together. There was also a rumbling sort of noise that could have been a very small volcano erupting in a pillarbox. There was also a sort of scratching noise – rather like a mouse the size of a rhinoceros trying not to frighten the cat.

Tom said to himself: 'If I didn't know better, I'd say it all sounded exactly as if we had a dinosaur living in our woodshed.'

So he climbed onto a crate, and looked through the woodshed window – and do you know what he saw?

'My hat!' exclaimed Tom. 'It's a Stegosaurus!'

He was pretty certain about it, and he also knew that although it looked ferocious, that particular dinosaur only ate plants. Nevertheless, just to be on the 29 safe side, he ran to his room, and looked up 'Stegosaurus' in one of his books on dinosaurs.

'I knew I was right!' he said, when he found it. Then he read through the bit about it being a vegetarian, and checked the archaeological evidence for that. It seemed pretty convincing.

'I just hope they're right,' muttered Tom to himself, as he unlocked the door of the woodshed. 'I mean after sixty million years, it would be dead easy to mistake a vegetarian for a flesh-eating monster!'

He opened the door of the woodshed *very* cautiously, and peered in.

The Stegosaurus certainly looked ferocious. It had great bony plates down its back, and vicious spikes on the end of its tail. On the other hand, it didn't look terribly well. Its head was resting on the floor, and a branch with strange leaves and red berries on it was sticking out of its mouth. The rumbling sound (like the volcano in the pillarbox) was coming from its stomach. Occasionally the Stegosaurus burped and groaned slightly.

'It's got indigestion,' said Tom to himself. 'Poor thing!' And he stepped right in and patted the Stegosaurus on the head.

This was a mistake.

The Stegosaurus may have been just a plant-eater, but it was also thirty feet long, and as soon as Tom touched it, it reared up onto its hind legs – taking most of the woodshed with it.

If the thing had looked pretty frightening when it was lying with its head on the floor, you can imagine how even more terrifying it was when it towered thirty feet above Tom.

'Don't be frightened!' said Tom to the Stegosaurus. 'I won't hurt you.'

The Stegosaurus gave a roar . . . well, actually it wasn't really a roar so much as an extremely loud bleat: 'Baaa -baaa -baaa!' it roared, and fell back on all fours. Tom only just managed to jump out of the way in time, as half the woodshed came crashing down with it, and splintered into pieces around the Stegosaurus. At the same time, the ground shook as the huge creature's head slumped back onto the floor.

Once again, Tom tried to pat it on the head. This time, the Stegosaurus remained where it was, but one lizard-like eye stared at Tom rather hard, and its tummy gave another rumble.

'You must have eaten something that disagreed 31

with you,' said Tom, and he picked up the branch that had been in the dinosaur's mouth.

'I've never seen berries like that before,' said Tom. The Stegosaurus looked at the branch balefully.

'Is this what gave you tummy-ache?' asked Tom.

The Stegosaurus turned away as Tom offered it the branch.

'You don't like it, do you?' said Tom. 'I wonder what they taste like?'

As Tom examined the strange red berries, he thought to himself: 'No one has tasted these berries for sixty million years . . . Probably no human being has *ever* tasted them.'

Somehow the temptation to try one of the berries was overwhelming, but Tom told himself not to be so stupid. If they'd given a huge creature like the Stegosaurus tummy-ache, they could well be deadly to a small animal like Tom. And yet . . . they looked so . . . *tempting* . . .

The Stegosaurus gave a low groan and shifted its head so it could look at Tom.

'Well, I wonder how you'd get on with twentieth-century vegetables?' said Tom, pulling up one of his father's turnips. He proffered it to the dinosaur. But the Stegosaurus turned its head away, and then –

quite suddenly and for no apparent reason — it bit Tom's other hand.

'Ouch!' exclaimed Tom, and hit the Stegosaurus on the nose with the turnip.

'Baaa!' roared the Stegosaurus, and bit the turnip.

Finding a bit of turnip in its mouth, the Stegosaurus started to chew it. Then suddenly it spat it all out.

'That's the trouble with you dinosaurs,' said Tom. 'You've got to learn to adapt . . . otherwise . . .'

Tom found himself looking at the strange red berries again.

'You see,' Tom began again to the Stegosaurus, 'We human beings are ready to change our habits . . . that's why we're so successful . . . we'll try different foods . . . in fact . . . I wonder what fruit from sixty million years ago tastes like? Hey! Stop that!'

The Stegosaurus was butting Tom's arm with its nose.

'You want to try something else?' asked Tom, and he pulled up a parsnip from the vegetable patch. But before he could get back to the Stegosaurus, it had lumbered to its feet and started to munch away at his father's prize rose-bushes.

'Hey! Don't do that! My dad'll go crazy!' shouted 33

Tom. But the Stegosaurus was making short work of the roses. And there was really nothing Tom could do about it.

He hit the Stegosaurus on the leg, but it merely flicked its huge tail, and Tom was lucky to escape as the bony spikes on the end missed him by inches.

'That's a deadly tail you've got there!' exclaimed Tom, and he decided to keep a respectable distance between himself and the monster.

It was at that moment that Tom suddenly did the craziest thing he'd ever done in his life. He couldn't explain later why he'd done it. He just did. He shouldn't have done, but he did . . . He pulled off one of the strange red berries and popped it into his mouth.

Now this is something you must never ever do – if you don't know what the berries are – because some berries, like Deadly Nightshade, are *really* poisonous.

But Tom pulled off one of the sixty-million-year-old berries, and ate it. It was very bitter, and he was just about to spit it out, when he noticed something wasn't quite right . . .

The garden was turning round. Tom was standing perfectly still, but the garden . . . indeed, as far as he 34 could see, the whole world . . . was turning around

and around, slowly at first, and then faster and faster
... until the whole world was spinning about him
like a whirlwind – faster and faster and faster and
everything began to blur together. At the same time
there was a roaring noise – as if all the sounds in the
world had been jumbled up together – louder and
faster and louder until there was a shriek! ... And
everything stopped. And Tom could once again see
where he was ... or, rather, where he wasn't ... for
the first thing he realized was that he was no longer
standing in his back garden ... or, if he was, he
couldn't see the remains of the woodshed, nor his
father's vegetable patch nor his house. Nor could he
see the Stegosaurus.

There was a bubbling pool of hot mud where the
rose-bushes should have been. And in place of the
house there was a forest of the tallest trees Tom had
ever seen. Over to his right, where the Joneses'
laundry line had been hanging, there was a steaming
jungle swamp.

But to Tom by far the most interesting thing was
the thing he found himself standing in. It was a sort
of crater scooped out of the ground, and it was
ringed with a dozen or so odd-shaped eggs.

'My hat!' said Tom to himself. 'I'm back in Jurassic

times! 150 million years ago! And, by the look of it, I'm standing right in a dinosaur's nest!'

At that moment he heard an ear-splitting screech, and a huge lizard came running out of the forest on its hind legs. It was heading straight for Tom! Well, Tom didn't wait to ask what time of day it was – he just turned and fled. But once he was running, he realized it was hopeless. He had about as much chance of out-running the lizard creature as he had of teaching it Latin (which, as he didn't even speak it himself, was pretty unlikely).

Tom had run no more than a couple of paces by the time the creature had reached the nest. Tom shut his eyes. The next second he knew he would feel the creature's hooked claws around his neck. But he kept on running . . . and running . . . and nothing happened.

Eventually, Tom turned to see his pursuer had stopped at the nest and was busy with something.

'It's eating the eggs!' exclaimed Tom. 'It's an egg-eater . . . an Oviraptor! I should have recognized it!'

But before he had a chance to kick himself, he felt his feet sinking beneath him, and an uncomfortably hot sensation ran up his legs. Tom looked down to
see that he'd run into the bog.

'Help!' shouted Tom. But the Oviraptor obviously knew as little English as it did Latin, and Tom felt his legs sliding deeper into the bubbling mud.

Tom looked up, and saw what looked like flying lizards gliding stiffly overhead. He wished he could grab onto one of those long tails and pull himself up out of the bog, but – even as he thought it – his legs slid in up to the knee. And now he suddenly realized the mud was not just hot – it was *boiling* hot!

His only chance was to grab a nearby fern frond. With his last ounce of strength, Tom lunged for it and managed to grab the end. The fern was tougher and stronger than modern ferns, but it also stung his hand. But he put up with it, and slowly and painfully, inch by inch, he managed to claw his way up the fern frond until he finally managed to pull himself free of the bog.

'This isn't any place for me!' exclaimed Tom, and, at that moment, the sky grew red – as if some distant volcano were erupting.

'Oh dear!' said Tom. 'How on earth do I get out of this?'

The moment he said it, however, he took it back, for the most wonderful thing happened. At least, it was wonderful for Tom, because he was particularly interested in these things.

He heard a terrible commotion in the forest. There was a crashing and roaring and twittering and bleating. A whole flock of Pterodactyls flew up out of the trees with hideous screeching. The lizard creature stopped eating the eggs and turned to look.

From out of the middle of the forest came the most terrible roar that Tom had ever heard in his life. The ground shook. The lizard thing screamed, dropped the egg it was devouring and ran off as fast as it could. Then out of the forest came another dinosaur, followed by another and another and another. Big ones, small ones, some running on four legs, some on two. All looking terrified and screeching and howling.

Tom shinned up a nearby tree to keep out of the way.

'Those are Ankylosaurs! Those are Pterosaurs! Triceratops! Iguanadons! Oh! And look: a Plateosaurus!'

Tom could scarcely believe his luck. 'Imagine seeing so many different kinds of dinosaur all at the same time!' he said to himself. 'I wonder where they're going?'

But the words were scarcely out of his mouth before he found out.

CRASH! Tom nearly fell out of the tree. CRASH! The ground shook, as suddenly – out of the forest – there emerged the most terrible creature Tom had ever seen or was ever likely to see again.

'Crumbs!' said Tom. 'I should have guessed! Tyrannosaurus Rex! My favourite dinosaur!'

The monster stepped out into the clearing. It was bigger than a house, and it strode on two massive legs. Its vicious teeth glowed red in the flaming light from the sky.

The curious thing was that Tom seemed to forget all his fear. He was so overawed by the sight of the greatest of all dinosaurs that he felt everything else was insignificant – including himself.

The next moment, however, all his fear returned with a vengeance, for the Tyrannosaurus Rex stopped as it drew level with the tree in which Tom was hiding. Its great head loomed just above Tom and the tree, and made them both quiver like jelly.

Before Tom knew what was happening, he suddenly saw the Tyrannosaurus reach out its foreclaws and pull the tree over towards itself. The next second, Tom found that the branch to which he was clinging 39 had been ripped off the tree, and he was being hoisted forty feet above the ground in the claws of the Tyrannosaurus Rex!

Tom was too terrified to be frightened. A sort of calm hit him as the creature turned him over and sniffed him – as if uncertain as to whether or not Tom was edible.

'He's going to find out pretty soon!' exclaimed Tom, as he felt himself lifted up towards those terrible jaws. 'I bet,' thought Tom, 'I'm the only boy in my school ever to have been eaten by his own favourite dinosaur!'

He could feel the monster's breath on his skin. He could see the glittering eye looking at him. He could sense the jaws were just opening to tear him to pieces, when . . . There was a dull thud.

The Tyrannosaurus's head jerked upright, and it twisted round, and Tom felt himself falling through the air.

The branch broke his fall, and as he picked himself up, he saw that something huge had landed on the Tyrannosaurus's back. The Tyrannosaurus had leapt around in surprise and was now tearing and ripping at the thing that had landed on it.

And now, as Tom gathered his wits, he suddenly realized what it was that had apparently fallen out of nowhere onto the flesh-eating monster. I wonder if you can guess what it was? ... It was Tom's old friend the Stegosaurus – complete with bits of the garden woodshed still stuck in its armour plates, and the branch of red berries sticking out of its mouth.

'It must have given up eating my dad's roses and gone back to the berries!' exclaimed Tom. And, at that very moment, Tom could have kicked himself. 'I'm an idiot!' he cried. For he suddenly noticed that the tree he'd climbed was none other than the very same magical tree – with its odd-shaped leaves and bright red berries.

But even as he reached out his hand to pick a berry that would send him back again in time, he found himself hurtling through the air, as the Tyrannosaurus's tail struck him on the back.

'Baaa!' bleated the Stegosaurus, as the Tyrannosaur clawed its side and blood poured onto the ground.

'Raaaa' roared the Tyrannosaur as the Stegosaurus thrashed it with the horny spikes on its tail.

The monsters reared up on their hind legs, and fought with tooth and bone and claw, and they swayed and teetered high above Tom's head, until the 41

Tyrannosaur lunged with its savage jaws, and ripped a huge piece of flesh from the Stegosaurus's side. The Stegosaurus began to topple . . . as if in slow motion . . . directly onto where Tom was crouching.

And Tom would most certainly have been crushed beneath the creature, had he not – at that very instant – found that in his hand he already had a broken spray of the red berries. And as the monster toppled over onto him, he popped a berry into his mouth and bit it.

Once again the world began to spin around him. The clashing dinosaurs, the forest, the bubbling mud swamp, the fiery sky – all whirled around him in a crescendo of noise and then . . . suddenly! . . . There he was back in his own garden. The Joneses' washing was still on the line. There was his house, and there was his father coming down the garden path towards him looking none too pleased.

'Dad!' yelled Tom. 'You'll never guess what's just happened!'

Tom's father looked at the wrecked woodshed, and the dug-up vegetable patch and then he looked at his prize roses scattered all over the garden. Then he looked at Tom:

'No, my lad,' he said, 'I don't suppose I can. But I'll tell you this . . . It had better be a *very* good story!'

NOTE: If you're wondering why the magical tree with the bright red berries has never been heard of again, well the Stegosaurus landed on it and smashed it, and I'm afraid it was the only one of its kind.

Oh! What happened to the Stegosaurus? Well, I'm happy to be able to tell you that it actually won its fight against the Tyrannosaurus Rex. It was, in fact, the only time a Stegosaurus ever beat a Tyrannosaur. This is mainly due to the fact that this particular Tyrannosaur suddenly got a terrible feeling of *déjà-vu* and had to run off and find its mummy for reassurance (because it was only a young Tyrannosaurus Rex after all). So the Stegosaurus went on to become the father of six healthy young Stegosauruses or Stegosauri, and Jurassic Tail-Thrashing Champion of what is now Surbiton!

Nicobobinus and the Doge of Venice

THIS is the story of the most extraordinary child who ever stuck his tongue out at the Prime Minister. His name was Nicobobinus [*Nick-Oh-Bob-In-Us*]. He lived a long time ago, in a city called Venice, and he could do anything.

Of course, not everybody knew he could do anything. In fact only his best friend, Rosie, knew he could, and nobody took any notice of anything Rosie said, because she was always having wild ideas anyway.

One day, for example, Rosie said to Nicobobinus: 'Let's put a rabbit down the Doge's trousers!'

'Don't be silly,' said Nicobobinus. 'The Doge doesn't wear trousers.'

'Yes he does,' said Rosie. '*And* we ought to boil his hat up and give it to the pigeons.'

'Anyway, who *is* the Doge?' asked Nicobobinus.

'How d'you know he doesn't wear trousers if you don't know who he is?' exclaimed Rosie (not unreasonably in my opinion).

Nicobobinus peered across the water and muttered: 'He doesn't live in the Doge's palace, does he?'

'Gosh!' said Rosie. 'I've never been fishing with a real genius before.'

'But he's the most important man in Venice!' exclaimed Nicobobinus.

'They've got universities for people like you, you know,' said Rosie, and she yanked a small carp out of the canal.

'What have you got against him?' asked Nicobobinus, as he watched her pulling out the hook with a well-practised twist.

'He's just extended his palace,' said Rosie, looking at her fish. It was about nine inches long.

'So?' said Nicobobinus, wondering why *he* never caught anything longer than his nose – which wasn't particularly long anyway.

'Well, he extended it all over my granny's house. That's what!' said Rosie.

'And now your poor old gran hasn't got anywhere to live?' asked Nicobobinus sympathetically.

'Oh yes she has! She's living with us, and I can't stand it!' replied Rosie.

Nicobobinus pretended, for a moment, that *he* had a bite. Then he said: 'But how will putting a rabbit down the Doge's trousers help?'

45

'It won't,' said Rosie. 'But it'll make me feel a lot better. Come on!'

'You don't really mean it?' gasped Nicobobinus.

'No,' said Rosie. 'We haven't got a rabbit – so it'll have to be a fish.'

'But that's our supper!' said Nicobobinus. 'And anyway, they've got guards and sentries and dogs all over the Doge's palace. We'd never get in.'

Rosie looked Nicobobinus straight in the eyes and said: 'Nicobobinus! It's *fun!*'

Some time later, when they were hiding under some nets on one of the little fishing boats that ferried people from the Giudecca to St Mark's Square, when the weather was too bad for fishing, Nicobobinus was still less certain.

'My granny says that where her kitchen used to be, they've built this fancy balcony,' Rosie was whispering, 'and she reckons any thief could climb in by day or night.'

'They drown thieves in the Grand Canal at midnight,' groaned Nicobobinus.

'They'll never catch us,' Rosie reassured him.

'Who's that under my nets?' shouted a voice.

'Leg it!' yelled Rosie, and she and Nicobobinus jumped overboard!

'Lucky we'd reached the shore!' panted Nicobobinus as the two sprinted across St Mark's Square.

'Hey! You two!' yelled the fisherman and gave chase.

Some time later, as Nicobobinus was standing on Rosie's shoulders pulling himself onto the balcony of the Doge's palace, he was even less certain.

'Have you got the fish?' hissed Rosie, as he pulled her up after him.

Nicobobinus could feel it wriggling inside his jerkin.

'No,' he replied. 'It was so unhappy I set it free. It said it didn't want to get caught by the Doge's guards in the company of two completely out-of-their-basket idiots like . . .'

'Look!' said Rosie. 'Do you see where we are?'

Nicobobinus peered into the room with Rosie and caught his breath. It was a magnificent room, with lacquered gold furniture and elegant paintings on the wall. But that wasn't what caught the attention of Rosie and Nicobobinus.

'Do you see?' exclaimed Rosie.

'Toys!' breathed Nicobobinus.

'We're in the nursery!' said Rosie, and she was. She had just climbed in.

Back at home Nicobobinus had just one toy. His uncle had made it for him, and, now he came to think about it, it was more of a plank than a toy. It had four wooden wheels, but the main part of it was definitely a plank. Rosie thought about her two toys, back in the little bare room where she slept with her sisters and her mother and her father and now her granny. One was moth-eaten (that was the doll that had been handed down from sister to sister) and the other was broken (that was a jug that she used to pretend was a crock of gold). But the Doge's children had: hoops, spinning tops, hobby horses, dolls' houses, dolls, toy furniture, masks, windmills, stilts (of various heights), rattles, building blocks, boxes, balls and a swing.

'There's only one thing,' whispered Rosie.

'What's that?' asked Nicobobinus as he picked up one of the hoops.

'The Doge hasn't got any children,' said Rosie, but before she could say anything else, one of them walked in through the door.

'Hasn't he?' said Nicobobinus.

'Well I didn't think he had,' said Rosie.

During this last exchange, the little girl who had just walked in through the door had turned pale, turned on her heel, and finally turned into a human cannonball, that streaked off back the way it had come.

'Quick!' cried Rosie. 'She'll give the alarm!'

And before Nicobobinus could stop her, Rosie was off in pursuit. So Nicobobinus followed . . . What else could he do?

Well, they hadn't got more than half-way across the adjoining room, when they both noticed it was rather full of people.

'Hi, everyone!' yelled Nicobobinus, because he couldn't think of anything else to say.

'That's torn it!' muttered Rosie. And on they dashed into the next chamber.

The Doge, who had been one of the people the room was full of, sat up in bed and said: 'Who are *they?*'

'I'll have them executed straightaway,' said the Prime Minister.

'No, no! *Apprehend* them,' said the Doge.

'At once,' said the Chief of the Guards.

'My clothes!' said the Doge, and sixteen people rushed forward with sixteen different bits of the

Doge's clothing. Getting out of bed for the Most Important Person In Venice in 1545 was a lot more elaborate than it is for you or me ... at least, it's more elaborate than the way I get up – I don't really know about you ...

Anyway, by this time, Nicobobinus and Rosie had bolted through six more rooms, down a flight of stairs and locked themselves in a cupboard.

'Phew!' said Rosie. 'Sorry about this.'

'That's all right,' said Nicobobinus.

'Please don't hurt me,' said a third voice. Nicobobinus and Rosie looked at each other in astonishment (although, as it was pitch-dark in the cupboard, neither of them realized they did).

'Who's that?' asked Nicobobinus.

'I'm not allowed to play with other children,' said the voice. 'My nurse says they might hurt me or kidnap me.'

'Don't be daft!' exclaimed Rosie. 'Children don't kidnap other children.'

'Don't they?' said the other occupant of the cupboard.

'No. And *we're* not going to hurt you,' said Nicobobinus.

'Then why are you here?'

'A lark,' said Rosie.

'What's that?' asked the girl.

'You know . . .' said Nicobobinus, 'fun.'

'Fun?' said the little girl. 'What's that?'

'Oh dear,' muttered Rosie.

'Stick with us and you'll see,' said Nicobobinus.

'All right,' said the girl. 'My name's Beatrice.'

But before either Nicobobinus or Rosie could tell Beatrice their names, there was a thundering as dozens of people went storming and clattering past the cupboard shouting things like: 'There they are!' and 'No! That's not them!' and 'Ow! Take that spear out of my ear!' and 'Quick! This way!' and 'Look in there!' and 'Help me! I've fallen over!' and so on.

When they'd all finally gone and it was quiet again, Nicobobinus, Rosie and their new friend stuck their heads out of the cupboard. The coast was clear, except for the guard who had fallen over.

'Give me a hand would you?' he asked. 'This armour's so heavy that once you fall over it's very difficult to get back on your feet again.'

'Doesn't that make it rather hard to fight in?' said Nicobobinus as they helped him to stand upright.

'Hopeless,' admitted the guard. 'But it *is* very 51

expensive. Now have you seen two children go past here?'

'Yes,' said Beatrice. 'They went that way!'

'Thanks!' said the guard and ran off as fast as his expensive armour would allow him. He'd got round the corner before he must have realized he'd made a mistake, for there was a crash and a muffled curse, as he tried to stop and turn, but fell over again instead.

'Come on!' yelled Rosie.

'Is this fun?' asked Beatrice, as they ran up another staircase and onto a long balcony and looked out over a narrow street.

'Are you enjoying it?' asked Nicobobinus.

'So-so,' said Beatrice.

'Then it's probably fun,' said Nicobobinus.

'Oh! Stop wittering, you two!' exclaimed Rosie. 'And help me down off here!' Rosie was already climbing over the balustrade and hanging from the balcony.

'That's too far a drop!' exclaimed Beatrice.

'You wait!' grinned Nicobobinus. 'We've done this before.' He whipped his belt off, and before you could say 'Venice and chips!' Rosie was clinging to the end, and being lowered down into the street.

52   'Oo-er!' said Beatrice.

'Come on!' called Rosie.

'Are you sure this is fun?' whispered Beatrice.

'Well it beats enjoying yourself!' shouted Nico-bobinus, as several guards suddenly appeared at the far end of the balcony.

'Hurry!' he said, and thrust the end of the belt into her hand.

'There they are!' shouted one of the guards. And without giving another thought, Beatrice followed Rosie down into the street.

'Nicobobinus!' yelled Rosie. 'How are *you* going to get down?'

'I'll be OK!' yelled Nicobobinus, although his main thought, as he ducked through a window, was actually 'Cripes!'

'I thought you'd done this before?' said Beatrice as she and Rosie legged it down the street.

'Well . . . maybe not from quite such a high balcony,' admitted Rosie, and they disappeared round the corner.

Nicobobinus meanwhile had made a discovery. He had discovered that the window that looked out onto the long balcony that looked over the Calle de San Marco was the window of the office of the Prime Minister. He also made a second discovery: it 53 was office hours. The Prime Minister was sitting on a sort of throne, holding an audience with several rather scruffy individuals who looked scared out of their wits.

'. . . and then take their heads off,' the Prime Minister was saying, as Nicobobinus backed in through the window and landed in front of him. 'Ah!' smiled the Prime Minister, signalling to his guards, 'another customer.'

Some time later, Nicobobinus found himself chained and shackled and being dragged into the Grand Audience Chamber of the Doge of Venice himself. It was a particularly magnificent room, and nowadays people come from all over the world to gaze up at the ornate ceiling and stare at the fine furnishings, while a guide talks too quickly in a language they can't understand and tells them about all the boring and pompous men and women with famous names that have come and gone through the doors of that famous place. But one story they never tell (and I don't know why) is the story I'm telling you now.

At that particular moment, however, the one thing Nicobobinus was *not* interested in was the magnificent decor of the Grand Audience Chamber. His one and only concern was how to get out again as quickly as possible (which, come to think of it, is probably what most of today's tourists are thinking too!).

'Bring the boy here,' yawned the Doge (who was actually wishing he was back in bed).

'We could start by simply cutting his feet off, and then move on up to his knees . . .' the Prime Minister was whispering in the Doge's ear as Nicobobinus was thrown onto the floor in front of them.

All eyes were upon him, and an excited buzz went around the Audience Chamber. The Doge looked at him and then said: 'What are your demands?'

Nicobobinus thought he hadn't heard right, so he said: 'I beg your pardon, Your Highness?'

'Where is she?' shrieked the Prime Minister, and suddenly everyone in the room was muttering and shouting the same thing.

'Silence!' commanded the Doge. Then he turned to Nicobobinus once more and said: 'You have kidnapped my daughter. I will give you what you want, providing you return her at once – unharmed.'

Nicobobinus was just about to say: 'No! I *haven't* kidnapped your daughter', but he didn't. Instead, he looked around at all the heavy, brooding faces, the wine-soaked noses and the sunken eyes of all the 55 important, pompous folk of Venice, and he said: 'I want one thing.'

'Yes?' said the Doge.

'And it isn't for me,' went on Nicobobinus.

'It's for your master,' assumed the Doge.

'No,' replied Nicobobinus, 'it's for your daughter.' A gasp went up around the room. 'It's something you must give Beatrice.'

The Doge couldn't speak for a moment, but eventually he managed to say: 'And what is it?'

'Fun,' said Nicobobinus.

'Fun?' said the Doge.

'Fun?' said all the pompous and important people of Venice.

'Fun!' said another voice, and there was Beatrice, the Doge's daughter, standing at the entrance to the Grand Audience Chamber, holding Rosie's hand. 'We've been having fun!'

Well, to cut a long story short, the Prime Minister still wanted to chop off Nicobobinus's and Rosie's heads and drown them in the Grand Canal at midnight, until the Lord Chief Advocate pointed out (after consulting various medical authorities) that you can't drown someone once you've cut their head off.

'Then just drown them like the rats they are!' exclaimed the Prime Minister.

'But they're only children,' said the Doge's mother.

'That's beside the point!' screamed the Prime Minister. 'It's the *principle* that matters! If you don't drown them, soon you'll have all the riff-raff of Venice climbing into the palace and making demands!'

But the Doge had fallen asleep, and his mother ordered that Beatrice should decide what was to become of Nicobobinus and Rosie. Beatrice said they had to come and play with her every Monday. And so that was that.

Later that evening, as the Doge was getting into bed, and all the assistants were gone, he said to his wife: 'You know my dear, a most extraordinary thing . . . Just now . . . Do you know what I found in my trousers?'

At about the same time, Nicobobinus and Rosie were sitting on Nicobobinus's doorstep laughing and laughing as Nicobobinus described how he had managed to slip the wriggling fish past the Doge's belt and into his trousers while the Doge's mother was kissing him goodnight.

'But one thing puzzles me,' said Rosie. 'When did you stick your tongue out at the Prime Minister?'

'I didn't,' replied Nicobobinus. 'That happened in a totally different adventure.'

'Was it the one where we set off to find the Land of Dragons?' asked Rosie.

'Ah!' said Nicobobinus. '*That* would be telling . . .'

Penguin Children's 60s

ALI BABA AND THE FORTY THIEVES • *Retold by N. J. Dawood*
THE AMAZING PIPPI LONGSTOCKING • *Astrid Lindgren*
ANNE AT GREEN GABLES • *L. M. Montgomery*
AT THE RIVER-GATES AND
OTHER SUPERNATURAL STORIES • *Philippa Pearce*
CLASSIC GHOST STORIES
CLASSIC NONSENSE VERSE
THE CLOCKWORK MOUSE • *Dick King-Smith*
DEAD MAN'S LANE • *Joan Aiken*
THE DRAGON ON THE ROOF • *Terry Jones*
FOUR GREAT GREEK MYTHS • *Roger Lancelyn Green*
THE GREAT MOUSE PLOT AND
OTHER TALES OF CHILDHOOD • *Roald Dahl*
THE GREAT TIME WARP ADVENTURE • *Jon Scieszka*
THE HOOLIGAN'S SHAMPOO • *Philip Ridley*
KEEP IT IN THE FAMILY • *Anne Fine*
KING ARTHUR'S COURT • *Roger Lancelyn Green*
THE LITTLE MERMAID AND
OTHER FAIRY TALES • *Hans Andersen (Translated by Naomi Lewis)*
LOST DOG AND OTHER STORIES • *Penelope Lively*
THE MIDNIGHT STORY • *Margaret Mahy*
MOOMINTROLLS AND FRIENDS • *Tove Jansson*
MRS PEPPERPOT TURNS DETECTIVE • *Alf Prøysen*
THE NIGHT TRAIN: STORIES IN PROSE AND VERSE • *Allan Ahlberg*
THE PIED PIPER OF HAMELIN AND OTHER CLASSIC STORIES IN VERSE
ROBIN HOOD AND HIS MERRY MEN • *Roger Lancelyn Green*
SHERLOCK HOLMES AND THE SPECKLED BAND • *Sir Arthur Conan Doyle*
SMACKING MY LIPS • *Michael Rosen*
TALES FROM ALICE IN WONDERLAND • *Lewis Carroll*
TALES FROM THE JUNGLE BOOK • *Rudyard Kipling*
THREE QUIRKY TAILS • *Paul Jennings*
TOM SAWYER'S PIRATE ADVENTURE • *Mark Twain*
TOM THUMB AND OTHER FAIRY TALES • *Jacob and Wilhelm Grimm*

Some other Puffin books by Terry Jones
Illustrated by Michael Foreman

FANTASTIC STORIES
FAIRY TALES
NICOBOBINUS
THE SAGA OF ERIK THE VIKING

Poetry

THE CURSE OF THE VAMPIRE'S SOCKS

Picture Books

THE BEAST WITH A THOUSAND TEETH
A FISH OF THE WORLD